Ajay wants to throw a ball straight and far. He tries, but he just can't do it. Then his friends remind Ajay how he learned to do other things. See what happens when they cheer him on.

Percy
Art Avenue
Emma
Sunny Street
Wide Way
Fire Station
Freda
Center Circle
Welcome to
SEE-AND-LEARN
City
Ready
Set
Pre-K
Ajay

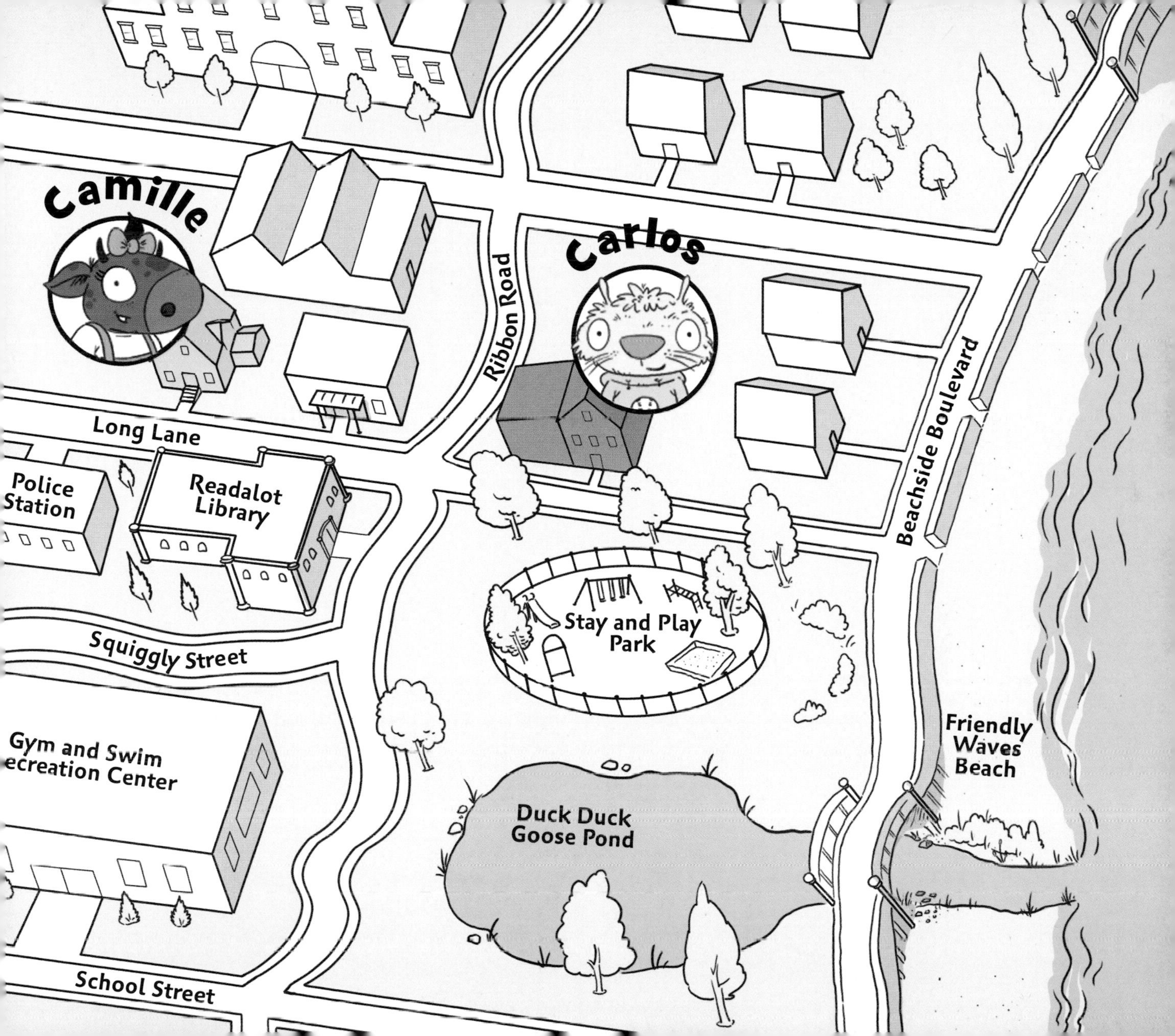
Camille
Carlos
Ribbon Road
Long Lane
Police Station
Readalot Library
Beachside Boulevard
Stay and Play Park
Squiggly Street
Gym and Swim
ecreation Center
Friendly Waves Beach
Duck Duck Goose Pond
School Street

Stuart J. Murphy

Good Job, Ajay!

Emotional Skills: Building Confidence

Charlesbridge

Ajay liked playing ball. But he couldn't throw the ball straight and far like Meera.

Ajay's older sister was really good at throwing a ball.

But when Ajay tried,

the ball didn't go straight.

And everybody laughed.

Percy and Freda came over to help Ajay practice.

Ajay threw the ball. It plopped down on his foot.
"I can't do it," said Ajay.
"Keep trying," said Percy. "It's like when you were trying to talk to Miss Cathy."

Ajay used to be shy about talking to his teacher.
He wanted to say things.
But they just didn't come out.

Then he tried saying something short.
"Hi, Miss Cathy," he whispered.
"Hi, Ajay," said Miss Cathy.
"What did you do last night?"

"I went to the store with my mommy,

and then I watched TV, and then . . ."

He was talking!

"Good job, Ajay," said Miss Cathy. "I'm glad you're using your words."

Ajay tried to throw the ball farther.
"You can do it," said Freda.

"This reminds me of when you were learning to swim," she said.

Ajay remembered.
Freda and Percy were really good at swimming.
Meera could even dive headfirst.

But Ajay was afraid to let go of the ladder.
"You can do it, Ajay," said Freda.

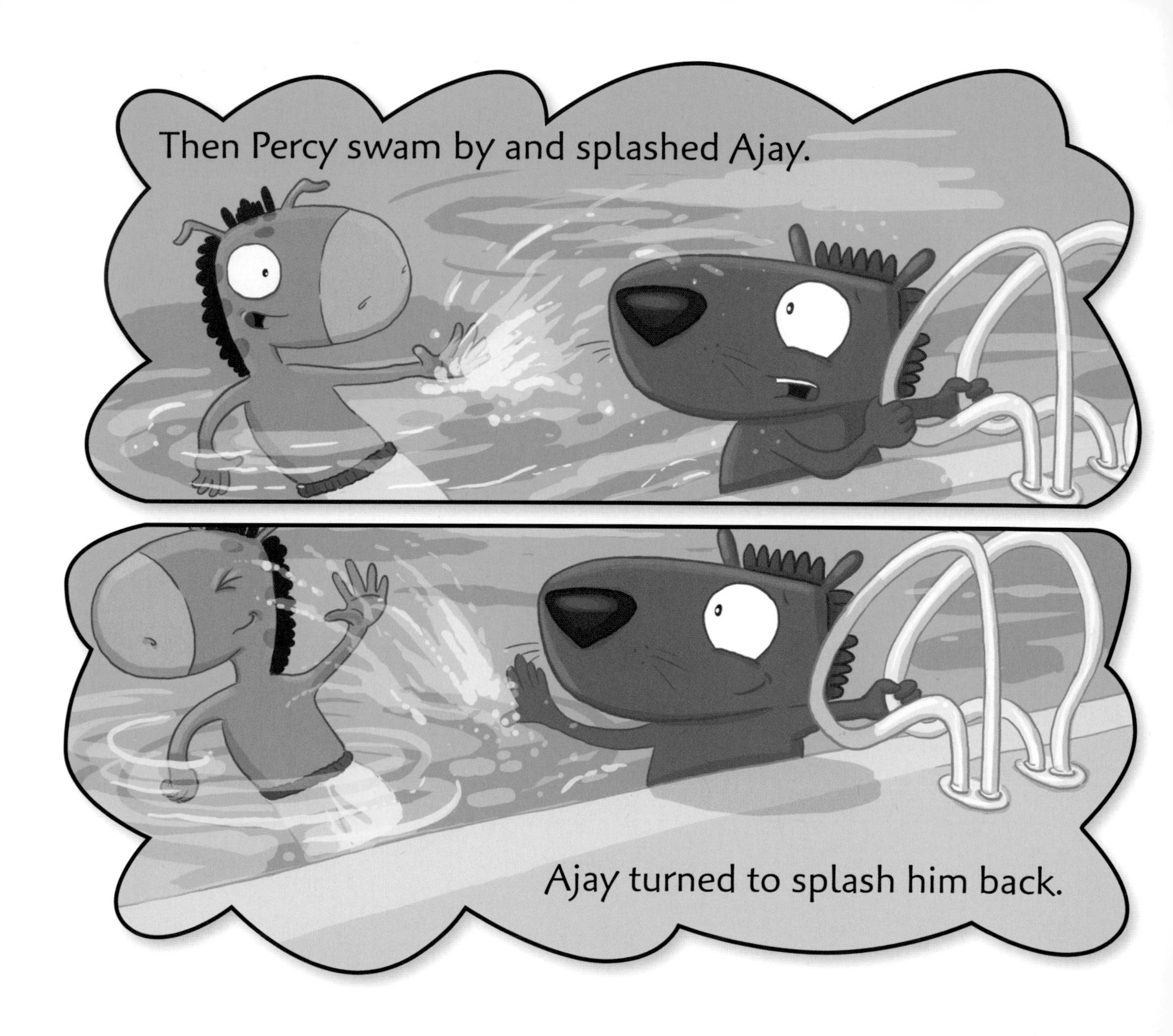
Then Percy swam by and splashed Ajay.
Ajay turned to splash him back.

He let go of the ladder. He kicked his feet.
He was swimming!
"Good job, Ajay," said Freda.
"I knew you could do it!"

Ajay tried to throw the ball harder.
"Keep throwing," said Percy.
"You're getting better," said Freda.

Meera came over to watch.
"I bet you still can't throw very far," she said.
"Oh, yeah?" said Ajay. "Just watch."

Ajay threw.

The ball went straight.

And everyone clapped. Even Meera.

“**Good job, Ajay!**” said Ajay.

Building Confidence

A Closer Look

1. How do **you** learn something new?
2. Look at the pictures in the story again. When did Ajay feel sad? How can you tell? Why was he sad?
3. When did Ajay feel happy? How can you tell? Why was he happy?
4. How do you help a friend who thinks something is too hard to do?
5. Draw a picture. Show how you feel when you have learned something new.

A Note About Visual Learning and Young Children

Visual Learning describes how we gather and process information from illustrations, diagrams, graphs, symbols, photographs, icons, and other visual models. Long before children can read—or even speak many words—they are able to assimilate visual information with ease. By the time they reach pre-kindergarten age (3–5), they are accomplished visual learners.

I SEE I LEARN™ books build on this natural talent, using inset pictures, diagrams, and highlighted words to help reinforce lessons conveyed through simple stories. The series covers social, emotional, health and safety, and cognitive skills.

Good Job, Ajay! focuses on building confidence, an emotional skill. Having confidence is critical as young children try new things, face new challenges, and attempt to reach higher goals.

Help your child take on something new!

Stuart J. Murphy is a Visual Learning specialist and the author of the award-winning MathStart series. He has also served as an author and consultant on a number of major educational programs. Stuart is a graduate of Rhode Island School of Design. He and his wife, Nancy, live in Boston, Massachusetts, near their children and three grandchildren, Jack, Madeleine, and Camille.

Published by Charlesbridge
85 Main Street
Watertown, MA 02472
(617) 926-0329
www.charlesbridge.com

Color separations by Chroma Graphics, Singapore
Manufactured by Regent Publishing Services, Hong Kong
Printed February 2010 in ShenZhen, Guangdong, China

Library of Congress Cataloging-in-Publication Data
Murphy, Stuart J., 1942–
Good job, Ajay! / Stuart J. Murphy.
p. cm. — (I see, I learn)
Summary: Ajay's friends encourage him as he practices throwing a ball. Includes questions about the text and notes to parents on visual learning.
ISBN 978-1-58089-454-8 (reinforced for library use)
ISBN 978-1-58089-455-5 (softcover)
[1. Encouragement—Fiction. 2. Persistence—Fiction.] I. Title. II. Series.
PZ7.M9563Go 2010
[E]—dc22 2009027567

Printed in China
(hc) 10 9 8 7 6 5 4 3 2 1
(sc) 10 9 8 7 6 5 4 3 2 1

teaches important skills for school readiness and daily life:

- **Social Skills**
- **Emotional Skills**
- **Health and Safety Skills**
- **Cognitive Skills**

Each book includes **A Closer Look:** two pages of activities and questions for further exploration.

Stuart J. Murphy is a Visual Learning specialist and the acclaimed author of the award-winning MathStart series.

www.iseeilearn.com

Charlesbridge
85 Main Street
Watertown, MA 02472
(617) 926-0329
www.charlesbridge.com